Okinba Launko

Ma'ami

Illustrated by
Chris Coady

CHELSEA HOUSE PUBLISHERS
New York • Philadelphia

Series Editor: Rod Nesbitt

This edition published 1995 by
Chelsea House Publishers, a division of Main Line Book Co.,
300 Park Avenue South, New York, N.Y. 10010
by arrangement with Heinemann

First published by Heinemann International Literature and Textbooks in 1994

ISBN 0-7910-3164-0

Printed and bound in Great Britain by
Cox & Wyman Ltd, Reading, Berkshire

1 3 5 7 9 10 8 6 4 2

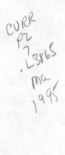

CONTENTS

CHAPTER ONE

It is cooler in our old house and half dark, and I sit inside and wait patiently. The walls and shelves that are so familiar seem bare now. And then I see the battered old tin, high up on one shelf. I take it down and in a moment the memories come flooding back. I am a small boy again, bursting with exciting news...

◇

I can't wait for my mother to come into the house. Instead I run towards her and jump at her just as she is trying to climb up on to the pavement. She has to struggle to keep her wrapper from falling off as I pull at her.

'Ma'ami! Ma'ami!' I am shouting. 'Ma'ami, look, I passed! I passed the examination and I was third in the class.'

I push the paper up at her so she can see it. She takes it, but has to make another effort to keep her balance. And then, I remember now, with sadness, that my mother cannot read. But she bends down, her face bright, all full of pride, and sweeps me up with one hand under my armpit, and carries me into the house.

She is crying with excitement now.

'My husband! My little husband! You, my own little boy! How proud I am! How you relieve all my pains! How you make all my work worth while. I want you to know, my little husband, that even if it takes all I have in this world, and even if it takes my life too in the end, you will complete your education, my little one.

'And those who say no, anyone who tries to stop me, should be careful for I have more strength than any of them! Ahh, you have killed me! Did you say third position in the class! My husband, I'll die first before you have to leave that school!'

She talks on for a few moments. She does not make much sense, but I listen quietly to what she is saying. And then she begins to sing. It is a song of happiness. At last she puts me down, pulls aside the long curtain dividing the room in two, and reaches across the wooden bed to push the window open. She turns to me.

'I left your food wrapped up in that cloth on the table. Have you eaten it?'

'No, Ma'ami, I haven't eaten. I was too excited, waiting to give you the news. Teacher says if I work hard and go on like this, I might get a scholarship next year.'

'You'll get it, my son! You will get it! The eyes of my father in his grave will never sleep. He'll go on watching over you and guard your steps. Whatever the obstacle, he will see you through! The prayer of the worm is that it can dance, and it dances! The prayer of the potato is to be sweet, and it is delicious! Ah, the prayer of the palm tree is to give birth to kernels, and it always bears them in abundance! My son, the future is what you want to make of it! I believe you can do anything you set your heart on. All your ambitions will come true if you work hard! But come, come and eat now!'

I sit down, and carefully undo the small bundle of folded cloth. Inside are two small dishes, one sitting neatly on top of the other. I lift up the one on top, and find the *eba* still steaming, under a cover of vegetable stew. As usual, there is no meat or fish, and I remember again that it is almost three years now since I last saw such a delicacy in our pot.

Ma'ami sees the disappointment in my eyes. She turns away quickly to pour out some water into a plastic bowl and then offers it to me.

'Come on,' she says. 'I'll help you wash your hands. The stew is good, you'll see!'

She sits on the edge of the bed which we share at night or on rainy afternoons when the day grows dark and the whole sky is growling and flashing its angry teeth at us. The storms do not frighten me, but I like to be near her when the thunder roars. I wash my hands in the bowl and she dries them with a towel lying on the bed. Her *gele* has begun to slip from her head, and as I look at her she takes it off to tie it again neatly.

'Eat your food, and stop staring, Big Eyes!' she scolds me. But she is smiling. I always love to see her hair, especially when, like now, it is done in these fine, delicate braids.

'You know what you're going to become?' she

asks. She gives me the answer herself immediately. 'Another Termogene! Yes, in a few years, you'll be just another Termogene!

'Maybe you don't know who it was that everyone called Termogene? He was a dangerous woman-chaser, who always caused a riot in the street any time he went for a walk. Oh, it was the funniest sight! You would see all the women running helter-skelter, dashing for the nearest place they could find to hide! Married women, single women, spinsters ... and particularly the virgins! Termogene was a demon! They said he had a ring on his third finger, which some people said he got from India. They said that if he just touched you with it, that was it! Whoever the woman, and however innocent, she would just turn and follow him straightaway. Ah, my little husband, you don't know how he frightened us! But some of the women looked after him anyway. I think some of them wanted to touch that ring.'

She starts to laugh at the memory, her eyes dancing. One or two braids escape from her *gele*. When she stops laughing, I shake my head at her.

'No, Ma'ami, I won't be like Termogene. It's just that you're a very beautiful woman. Even more beautiful than our teacher, Mrs Edun. But she is very beautiful too. I'm going to marry her when I grow up.'

'Oh I see! So you're going to marry her! And what about her husband then? What will he say to that when you go to marry her?'

'He doesn't love her. He beats her. Sometimes he beats her in the morning before she comes to school. I know that, because she is always crying when she arrives in school. But when I marry her– '

'Eat your food!' Ma'ami says. 'Look at you, choosing a wife already! Do you know how old you are?'

'Yes, of course!' I say. 'I know exactly how old I am. I'll be ten tomorrow!'

There is a silence, during which I watch Ma'ami clutch her *buba*. Her eyes grow bigger and bigger, as her lips begin to move silently.

'Great God!' she exclaims at last. 'It's true! It's tomorrow! Your birthday is tomorrow.'

She throws her arms up into the air and joins the hands above her head.

'Tomorrow's your birthday!' she shouts. 'Oh my God, how could I have forgotten?'

She gets up after a while, climbs on our small stool, and reaches for an old rusty Ovaltine tin on a shelf behind the bed. She brings it down, and then goes and finds a knife which she uses as a lever to open the tin. The lid flies off and rolls from the bed on to the floor with a clatter. I reach down quickly and snatch it before it rolls under the bed.

Ma'ami empties the contents of the tin on the bed. Some papers fall out, small, wrinkled sheets. Then other odds and ends, all kinds of small wrappings which I know to contain items varying from powdered medicines to earrings and glass beads.

Ma'ami empties the contents of the tin on the bed.

Sometimes there are small coins and banknotes too. This tin is both her pharmacy, and her bank for valuables and other keepsakes, and for money she does not wish to spend yet.

She begins to select and search now, but only two coins, a ten kobo and a five kobo piece, fall out from among the wrappings.

Ma'ami sighs deeply, puts the papers and wrappings back into the tin, and slams the lid on again angrily.

For a while she sits there, the coins in her palm, and a faraway look in her eyes. Then her lips begin to move silently again, as if she is having an argument with herself. In the half-dark room, I am still able to see the beads of sweat gathering in a broken line along her upper lip. Then she seems to wake up again.

'My little husband,' she asks with a weak smile, 'what would you like me to give you tomorrow? You have done so brilliantly in class, and again, it's your birthday. So it's a double celebration! Tell me, what do you want for a gift?'

I think for a moment, then I say, 'Meat, Ma'ami!'

Her head jerks forward suddenly, as if she has just stepped on a thorn. Something like a little fire starts to gleam in her eyes.

'What did you say?'

'I want meat, Ma'ami. Please buy me some meat tomorrow.'

'Meat!' she cries. 'What nonsense! Haven't I told

you before? I can't afford it! Don't you understand? Where would I find the money?'

Her palm slams down on the Ovaltine tin, making it leap like a toad across the bed. The sound makes my heart jump up into my throat. I dare not look at her.

'It's hard enough, just finding something to fill your stomach every day,' she shouts. 'And now you're asking for meat! How am I going to get meat? Do you want me to go out and steal it? Ehn? Is that what you want? Do you want me to go out and begin to steal?'

She gives a long angry hiss, as she stands up, towering and quivering above me like a whip.

'You saw it, when the government people closed down all the stalls in the market. They destroyed my stall and seized my goods. The rogues! Yes, yes, yes, I know that most of the other sellers have got their stalls back, after seeing the officers in charge. But I have sworn I will not see anybody, and I know now I won't get my stall again. Perhaps I will be the only person in the whole market not to get her stall back. Because I know how the others got their stalls back. They let those rogues make love to them. But I will never sell my body! I'll never agree to sleep with a man I don't love. What for? I can't, and I won't, and that's that. My father did not raise me up to be a prostitute. Or is that what you would like your mother to be, one of those women they laugh at in the street? No! No! Never, you hear? Never. So where do you expect me to find the money to buy meat?'

She is stamping her feet now, her eyes are shining and her arms are swinging wildly about.

'Meat! At the price it costs nowadays. You know something, my little husband? We haven't even paid our rent here for months! Yes, that's the truth! And the landlord, he's only taking pity on us for now, because of you. Because he says you're a nice boy, and he likes you. But how long do you think we'll be able to depend on that? How long do you think his patience will last? Every day I have to be careful when I go out into the street. I have to make sure that I don't run into him. I have to avoid him all the time, like a thief. And do you know, now they are saying, the Town Council people are saying, that we are going to have to start paying for the water we use. Water! And don't forget that I still have to pay your school fees for next term. Ah, some children are just never grateful for anything. Meat! Meat! If you want meat so badly, why don't you go to your father and ask him for meat?'

She has been rushing round the room, throwing things furiously about, while I am cringing in terror under the far corner of the bed, the pillow round my head. I have never seen her like this before. And where would I find my father?

Now, exhausted, she throws herself on the bed, heavily, as if to try and hurt herself. There is a loud bang as she falls on the mattress and the bed crashes against the wall. Then Ma'ami bursts out crying noisily. I decide to seize the chance. I throw down the pillow and race quickly out of the room.

Kokumo and the others are playing football with a sucked-dry orange in front of the house. They call to me, but I don't answer them. My heart is thumping so much that I am afraid it will burst if I don't hold it with my hands. I want to get as far away as possible from the boys and sit by myself, looking, but not seeing anything. I run down the street and around the corner. I sit beside an old tree feeling very sad and lonely. It is only after a while that I realise, with surprise, that it is my voice that I can hear crying, and my tears wetting my shirt.

Then I hear steps coming behind me on the pavement. Even without turning, I know who it is. She comes and sits beside me, and puts her arms round me. Delicately she unfolds the edge of her *gele* and wipes my eyes.

She wraps her arms round me again. 'My little husband, you poor, poor thing!'

I throw my hands out, and collapse on her lap. Only then does my heart stop thumping. Her arms are the only shelter I know. All my fears suddenly disappear in a moment.

'My little son,' she is saying softly into my ears, 'please stop crying. Forgive me. I'm sorry. Ah, poverty. It's poverty, this always not having any money, that makes me act like this, saying such harsh words to my little darling. Poverty, and bitterness, the bitter memory that it was not always like this.

'I remember all my relatives, my father's brother especially, the one I lived with after my father died,

Her arms are the only shelter I know.

warning me against marrying your father. They insisted I should finish my education first, then think of marriage afterwards. But love! Love makes you do foolish things when you're young.

'All my friends, all young like me, they cheered me on, urged me not to lose such a dashing young man. And so I didn't listen to my family.

'And now here we are, you and me. I doubt if your father even remembers us any more. He's got so many other women, and other children. But I'm sorry, no more of that. You're too young to be burdened with all this. Maybe one day you'll understand. But let's forget it all for now. Tomorrow, and I am swearing it to you, tomorrow you will eat meat in this house.'

'No, Ma'ami,' I reply. 'I don't want it any more. I didn't know it would hurt you.'

'Nonsense,' she says and stands up. 'You just wait for me. I am going out now, and as soon as I come back, we shall see.'

'You're going out?'

'Yes. I'm a woman, remember? And as you always say, with those Termogene eyes of yours, your mother is still pretty!' She laughs, but I don't like it. Then she digs her fingers into my ribs, forcing me to laugh too. 'One day you'll know, my little husband. Pretty women, they can always find the means, when they want something badly. As long as their conscience doesn't get in the way. Wait for me, I'll soon be back.'

As she is about to leave, she turns, and puts the ten kobo coin in my hand.

'While I'm gone,' she says, 'go and buy yourself some groundnuts.'

I stand there and watch her walking away. Where is she going? And what does she mean by 'as long as their conscience doesn't get in the way'? Who, or what, is this conscience? I stand there, watching her walk away.

CHAPTER TWO

I stand for a while, thinking about what she has said, watching her as she walks away. And then, as she crosses the gutter over by Baba Ajao's house, I make up my mind. I jump down from the pavement, and I begin to run after her.

She is walking at a very fast pace, her gaze fixed in front of her, and does not even look back once. She spots a bus and starts to wave for it to stop. It is only when the *danfo* bus pulls up beside her, and she turns to enter, that she sees me at her elbow.

'My little husband!' she exclaims. 'What are you doing here? Where are you going?'

'I'm going with you, Ma'ami!'

Her eyes open wide in her familiar look of surprise. 'You're going with me. And do you know where I'm going?'

The bus conductor shouts, and there are a few other growls of impatience from inside the bus. The driver makes the engine run faster. It makes a long vroom-vroom-vroom. He looks back and waves angrily. He is about to drive off.

'Wait!' shouts Ma'ami, putting a foot inside the bus. 'Please wait for me.' Then she turns to me. 'Get back to the house at once.'

I say nothing. But just as the bus is about to move off, I jump inside, holding on to the conductor's khaki trousers and the exposed iron frame of one of the seats. The *danfo* boy, frightened, reaches out hastily to pull me inside, shouting angry words at me. But I don't mind the abuse. Then he slams the door shut, and we are off.

For a while Ma'ami does not say anything. I look quickly at her from the corner of my eye. I am not brave enough to look at her directly. I can see her lips twitching as they do occasionally when she is boiling with rage. Still she says nothing.

From time to time the bus stops. Some of the passengers get off, others jump on. Then the bus moves on again.

There are lots of different noises all around us. I can hear the screaming calls of the *danfo* boy and the driver shouting and cursing. There are the sudden outbursts of quarrelling or of laughter among the passengers. I can hear the shouts of stall owners and of travelling evangelists along the road, and the unhappy chants of the beggars at the windows, especially at the road junctions. There is a lot of noise in the evening and everywhere people are coming home from work or shopping for food for the evening meal.

But Ma'ami alone says nothing. Her lips are no longer twitching, but a broken line of sweat has built along the tip of her upper lip, like strange decorative beads.

Then, just as the bus comes to the railway crossing by the new market, Ma'ami, catching everybody by surprise, suddenly lets out a piercing scream.

16

'Yeah! Yeah-pah!' she shouts loudly. 'My wallet! It's gone! Gone! Someone has taken my wallet. Oh, they have killed me today!'

'What? What's happened?' The voices of several of the passengers call from all around her.

'My wallet! Didn't you hear me, you thieves? I had my wallet tied up, right here! See!' She pulls out the edge of her wrapper, showing where it has been neatly cut. 'Someone's taken it. Someone in this bus, who will never be happy again in this life! Ah, this world! This world!'

As eyes begin to shift to them, the two passengers sitting directly next to Ma'ami begin to shout too now, crying that they are innocent. They offer to be searched. They call down the most terrible curses on their own heads if they are indeed guilty of stealing anybody's wallet.

The bus comes to a complete stop by the side of the road. Ma'ami pushes her way through, and leaps down on to the grass beside the road, pouring out a stream of curses. I get down too, to stand behind her. But she has already started to scream and moan and is rolling in the grass.

'Ah, this world, this terrible world! The little money I had. It was money I was just going to use to buy some food for this poor son of mine, and my twins at home.' She twists and turns on the ground, waving her arms and shouting. 'There must be no God any more! The god of my son and the gods of the twins are no longer the good caring gods they used to be. If they were, this thief would not get away like this, without getting punished for it. Ah, how can some people be so wicked? How will I feed these children now?'

She goes on and on, while all kinds of voices are trying to cut in, soothe her and offer her help. Many pairs of hands are trying to lift her back to her feet. But it is all in vain. She will not stop twisting and rolling and calling out in a loud voice. Ma'ami has done all this before. I know because I have seen her do it. She does it very well, and has practised it on many people in the past. She tears off her *gele*, lets it fall over her shoulders, and then to the ground. She allows herself to be pulled up, but promptly crashes back to the ground.

More passengers climb down, pleading. 'Get up now, *mama ibeji*! Please get up!'

I almost laugh. Where are those twins at home? But I squeeze my face up so as not to betray her.

'Please stand up now and get back into the bus,' a woman says to Ma'ami. 'Remember, God is always there! He won't forget your twins. Anyone who dares to steal from twins will be punished by God. Whoever has stolen your money is going to receive a terrible punishment. I feel sorry for him. Now please, stop crying!'

Then a voice comes in above the others. 'Come, my dear woman. This is your son, isn't he? He will not starve today, by the grace of Allah! Let him take this!'

18

I hold out my hand, and a coin is dropped into my palm. Then one by one other passengers come up and put money in my hand.

Ma'ami gradually stops crying, but nothing will persuade her to climb back into the bus. The crowd of passers-by which has gathered around us add their voices, but Ma'ami just shakes her head silently.

'Please come back into the bus,' two women say.

'No, no, thank you all very much,' Ma'ami says quietly. 'But after what's happened, I can't trust myself in that bus again. Please understand. I do appreciate your kindness. The heads of my twins will bless you all. But we'll find another bus. I won't put my child inside that one again!'

'Well, that's okay,' shouts the *danfo* boy, 'but what about the fare?'

'Come, here's my neck. Why don't you cut my head off? Fare indeed! Maybe it was you who stole my wallet! Just look at his eyes. Maybe he was the one who took my wallet.'

The *danfo* conductor shouts back, but the crowd is with Ma'ami. A chorus of shouts silences the boy and his driver, and finally the bus starts up and drives off without us. Ma'ami rearranges her dress and then takes my hand. We begin to walk back towards the cattle market by the rail crossing. The crowd is still watching us.

'How much do you have in your hand?' she asks after we have left them all behind.

I open my fist and pour the coins into her hand. I

I open my fist and pour the coins into her hand.

feel so bad I cannot talk. How could she behave like that? How could she take their money?

She looks at me, reading my face. Then she counts the money.

'Fifty-three kobo, hmm. It will take us back at least, so we won't have to walk home. But it's still not enough to buy your meat, my husband.'

We stop by the big Mobil sign while she thinks. I am still too full of emotion to say anything. I concentrate on looking at the cars flashing past, and on the handsome people inside them. One day, I know, I'm going to be a pop star, with my own car, and lots of beautiful girls. And I'm going to build a huge palace for Ma'ami, and buy her the largest Mercedes Benz car in the world, with automatic power and everything. Then she will never again have to do a disgraceful dance for *danfo* drivers.

She taps me on the shoulder.

'How do I look now, my husband?'

She has put her *gele* on at an angle, making her look even more beautiful. But I refuse to tell her. I just look away.

'You won't talk to me? Okay, but remember, I never asked you to come along. If you had stayed at home I could have managed just as well. Now just wait here, I'll come back in a minute.'

A car has pulled up at one of the petrol pumps, and a fat man has rolled out of it. He begins to give instructions to the attendants.

I watch Ma'ami go up to him and greet him with a

brief curtsey. And I realise, with a sick feeling in my stomach, that another of the little acts she uses to get money is starting.

'Good evening, sir! ... I am Mrs Jeboda ... You don't remember me? ... Your wife, we were together in primary school ... yes, so long ago, sir! ... I'm fine, thank you! ... And that's my son over there ... Oh just a little problem, sir ... and I'm sorry to have to bother you ... But when I saw you come out of this car just now, I said, praise God, how lucky ...'

'What's the problem, madam?'

'You see, sir ... we came to the market to buy some meat, me and my son. We took a *danfo*, and as I've always done all my life, I tied up my wallet here.' She shows the fat man the edge of her wrapper with the slash in it. 'I'm sorry, I don't like to be bothering you, but you see ... I tried my best! Yes, I did, but I just don't know how the thief managed, sir. Now, no meat, no wallet, not even the money to get back home.' She begins to sob. 'And I'm reduced to begging for help from a stranger.'

'Madam, stop, it's not the end of the world ...' The fat man does not know what to do. He starts to walk backwards.

'All my month's salary, sir. And the boy has no father either!' I can hear her from where I am watching. I sigh sadly, remembering the jibes from my playmates and their boasts about their fathers.

But of course Ma'ami does not notice, as she

continues her wailing. 'Yes, sir, since I lost my husband, that salary is all we've had to depend on. And then, today ...' Her cries rise again, choking off the words.

'Come, come, I said I'll help! And I'm not really a stranger, am I, if you were at school with my wife? Come, Mrs er, Jeboda ... It's just a pity that I don't have much on me now, I'm on my way to play tennis at the club down the road, as you can see ... But please, this will help ...'

Ma'ami goes down on her knees. She starts to pray out loud for the man, not stopping till he has driven off. Then she walks back towards me, almost bouncing on her feet and running as she counts the money.

'Twenty-five naira!' she shouts, waving the notes in the air and laughing merrily. 'A whole twenty-five naira! I can't believe it! Just imagine! Now, my little husband, is it just cow meat you want tomorrow for your birthday, or shall we try for an elephant?'

Her laughter rings out. It is sweet, like a bell. Then she looks at me for the first time, and sees the tears running freely down my cheeks.

'Tears, my husband!' She folds up the money and tucks it into the front of her wrapper. There is a long silence, during which I try as hard as I can, but I cannot stop crying. Then suddenly Ma'ami stoops down and hugs me hard to her breast.

'My husband,' she says softly, 'you don't want your

mother to start crying too, in public, do you? So please, stop. Stop ... You know I tried. Yes, what didn't I try, after they knocked my stall down, to earn money by honest means? I tried everywhere ... but there are no jobs anywhere. Even people who have jobs are told every day that their jobs are finished. No one's sure any more what will happen tomorrow. It's the way the army are governing us. They said they were going to correct all the bad things which had happened in the past. They said they were going to chase away all those terrible politicians who did nothing but steal our money. But look at what has happened. There is hunger everywhere. That's what the army government has brought us. Men out of work, young people wasting away in the streets. My husband, it's as if there's some terrible plague upon us. You understand, don't you? Think, my little one. If it's so difficult for men, imagine what it is like for a woman! I swore I would not sell my body like others, but today ... yes, today, when I saw your eyes ... If you hadn't followed me out, I don't know. Perhaps in the end, just to get you some meat ... perhaps ...'

Her voice quivers, dies into a whisper. But she recovers quickly. 'Tears! What good are tears? Tears are for the rich, they don't help poor people like us! Come, we must be strong, you hear. Even when we have to roll our pride a bit on the ground, as you see me do sometimes, putting on these acts. As long as I am able to put something every day in your stomach, without losing my honour. Come on, race me, you lazy bones! Let's see who gets to that lamp post over there first!'

It's our favourite game. I jump up and race after her. She already has a slight advantage, but I know I will reach the post before her.

CHAPTER THREE

Evening is approaching rapidly, and the sky is darkening all around us. We still haven't bought the meat. We have gone through the meat stalls a number of times, feeling and pricing the various chunks on display, but Ma'ami is not satisfied.

She takes my hand. 'My husband,' she says, 'I think we should go home, and come back tomorrow. You see all this meat in the market? Yesterday I would have crawled on my belly to have just a piece of it. But now, my husband, I'm sure it's all stale meat, the left-overs that the butchers have not been able to sell. And who knows, some of it may even be dog meat, or camel. It's all so cheap, so tempting. But touch it, you see how soft it all is? No, no, my husband, let's save our money and, first thing tomorrow morning, I'll be back here. Yes, as soon as you're off to school. I will be the first person they'll see here tomorrow.'

She leads me through the wooden stalls where some of the traders are already packing up, and then out on to the tarred road.

There is a lot of movement on the street. Many of the women who own the stalls are going home too. Different groups are walking along in files, as if they are part of a long procession. Their children walk in front, carrying bundles on their heads. I see that many of the children are even younger than me, and I begin to envy them their lives in the market. Working

Along the road a large brown cow is running towards us.

there seems to be dangerous and exciting, and therefore better than my life at school.

Suddenly there are shouts and screams from the road ahead of us. Then, all around us, people begin to shout and run helter-skelter, flinging their arms in the air. Ma'ami pulls me quickly off the road, and pushes me down behind a pile of stones. With great excitement, we watch the drama which has caused the people to run away and leave the street empty. Along the road a large brown cow is running towards us with a broken rope dangling from its neck. The people who are chasing it run and fall and pick themselves up again. As they try to catch it, the cow kicks and dodges and moos angrily back at them.

But the cow really has no chance. They catch it at last, twist the rope sideways and bring the cow crashing down. There is loud applause from all the watchers. Finally the street is safe again.

'That's what life is all about,' says Ma'ami with a sigh, as we stand and brush the dust off our clothes. 'Yes, that's how our life is. It's all a game. Some want to eat, some end up being eaten, and some are there just watching and clapping.'

I look at her. I don't understand. Ma'ami laughs, ruffling my hair.

'No, I don't expect you to understand. Not yet. But some day soon, my husband, some day soon...'

We get to the bus stop. Or rather to the place by the roadside where many people are standing and waiting. There is already a large crowd, I notice, and as we wait other people arrive to join us. We wait there for a long time, but there is no bus in sight.

We wait and wait, and the crowd keeps growing. Sometimes, however, one or two people pull out, shouting and waving their hands, and declaring that they will make the journey on foot. There is a lot of talking and we grow slowly impatient and stamp our feet on the sand.

Someone begins to accuse the government, and especially the Minister of Transport. I ask Ma'ami who the minister is but she just laughs.

'How do you expect someone like me to know, my husband? Such big men live far, far away from little people like us. It's one of the reasons we send you off to school, so that you'll go and find out the names of our leaders. They are the ones who remember us only when they want our votes or our taxes.' She laughs again, patting my head.

But someone else is speaking in defence of the government.

He says that it is not the fault of the ministers who are now in government. It is the fault of the politicians who were there before them. This statement starts an argument which becomes angrier and angrier. I start to think that they are going to fight, and I cling closer to Ma'ami.

But, just at that moment, another voice speaks up from the back of the queue.

'You people are stupid! What are you complaining about? Didn't you hear the minister talking last week on the radio? He said a good, happy life is not for poor people! That's what he said. So who said the bus was for ordinary people like you? If a bus comes it will only be because the minister has been kind.'

For some reason everyone starts to laugh and laugh. The fight which was about to start has been forgotten, and the argument ends.

My feet are aching. Ma'ami bends down, pretends to lift me up, and then collapses.

'Yeh, what is this?' she shouts in alarm. 'You're so heavy. What has my husband been eating? Surely not only what I've been feeding you. It has to be more than that. Aha, maybe it's that woman, the one you're going to marry – what's her name again?'

'Mrs Edun.' I give her the answer promptly, with great pleasure.

'Ah yes, Mrs Edun, your sweetheart. Maybe she has been feeding you behind my back.'

'Well,' I say proudly, 'she buys me groundnuts and *boole* now and then.'

'I knew it. You are going to be just like Termogene, if not worse. Taking gifts from women in secret ... Ah, there's the bus at last!'

An old, rickety bus, puffing out black smoke like a fireplace on which rain has fallen, and panting like a dying old man, rumbles to a stop. An immediate scramble begins as all of us rush forward at once. It grows into a furious fight, with some of the passengers inside the bus trying to get off, while those outside push to get in through the same doors.

And it soon becomes obvious that Ma'ami and I have no chance at all. The men are pushing the women to one side as they struggle to climb into the bus. The children are standing back, looking frightened.

Through all the noise I hear Ma'ami shout at me, 'Hey, my husband, can you find your way home alone?'

I look at her in surprise. I do not understand the question.

'Hey, answer me! Will you know where to get off by yourself? Look, if I give you some money, maybe you can slip in under these people, and get into the bus. You'll know where to get off, won't you? I'll follow you on foot, and be with you later. Is that okay?'

I look up into the swirl of clothes and limbs, and I see her face, covered all over in sweat. I shake my head. 'No, Ma'ami,' I say, 'I'll walk with you.'

We pull back, exhausted, from the crowd. The bus leaves, leaning dangerously to one side and coughing out its smoke again. With the heads of several passengers hanging out of its doors and windows at various angles, the bus reminds me of one of those monsters in Ma'ami's stories.

We wait a little more, but no bus comes. It is night now and the lights begin to come on at the Mobil station far away in the distance, flashing out one after another, like eyes opening to see in the darkness.

'Come on,' says Ma'ami, 'it doesn't look as if these *danfos* are going to come again today. For all you know, the police may have chosen this evening to check their driving licences and papers or something. It's still too far for you to walk. And with Mrs Edun's food in your belly, you've grown too heavy for me to carry!'

'What will we do, then?' I ask.

'Fly,' she says, laughing and starting to run. She opens her arms out wide, and begins to flap them up and down. Then, turning, she begins to run faster. 'I'm flying away, whoo-oosh! Catch me if you can.'

I spread out my arms too, and run after her, making bird noises.

I am completely out of breath when we stop at the petrol station, panting.

'All right, my dear Termogene,' says Ma'ami. 'I can see you're exhausted already! You may be able to make women think you are wonderful, but you wouldn't do too well as a bird, I'm afraid. So, suppose we do something reckless? Suppose we take a taxi!'

My eyes light up. My heart is beating uncontrollably. Me, inside a taxi! Ride in a car. What a dream! How those boys will be so envious when they see me getting down. They're always boasting about their fathers, and laughing at me. I will now have something to make them jealous. After all, none of their fathers has ever entered a car before. Now they will see. They will see that even a boy who hasn't a father can become the hero of the street.

Ma'ami reads my mind. 'It's a dream, my husband.

And I can tell you I've never been inside one myself. But it's our special day, isn't it? And tomorrow will be even bigger. So why don't we do it? We've got the money, and we have to get home.'

It takes us some time, but we finally get a taxi willing to go our way. Ma'ami goes into some haggling with the driver over the fare, and then we get in. The dream begins.

There are two men already inside the taxi, one in front beside the driver, and the other at the back. Ma'ami and I climb into the back seat, and we move off.

It is wonderful, wonderful. A number of times Ma'ami has to warn me to sit down and stop jumping on the seat, as I stand up to wave at passers-by. But I want the whole world to see me, to remember me. It is just too bad that none of those we pass seems to notice or care. Perhaps they are too jealous of me.

The car stops suddenly. There are two new passengers waiting to come in. As there is space for only one more person, however, the driver turns to appeal to Ma'ami.

'Please, my pretty woman, help me. Let your small brother come over and sit at the front here with me. Then these two people can join you at the back. God will reward you for your kindness.'

Ma'ami is obviously pleased to be taken for my sister rather than my mother. She smiles and asks me to climb over. I don't mind at all. I am even more excited to be at the front, close to the driver. Now I can watch the movements he makes to start the car and then keep it on the road.

I am watching the driver so closely that what happens next catches me by complete surprise. We have not gone far at all when suddenly I see the driver's foot jam down on the pedal as he shouts something to the other passengers. The car jerks to a stop, and I am thrown forward. My head hits the dashboard and I fall on the floor of the car. Then, almost at the same moment, the door on my side is thrown open, and I find myself flying out headlong into the darkness of the night. I land on my face with a crash. All the breath is knocked out of me. And then, through the pain, I am hearing other screams, and the screech of tyres and the banging of doors.

Finally I emerge from some kind of blackness, and there is a voice shouting down at me.

'My husband! My little husband! Answer me. Answer me!'

I try to say something, but my voice seems to be lost somewhere far away. And then, quite suddenly, I am awake, and I recognise the hands of my mother holding my face.

I open my eyes, and she is leaning over me, her clothes lying open. The straps of her underskirt are hanging down broken, and I can see one of her breasts like a brown pawpaw fruit through her torn *buba*. Her hair is all dishevelled, and her face is bleeding in a number of places.

But as soon as I open my eyes, Ma'ami sweeps me

I find myself flying out headlong into the darkness of the night.

up to her breast with a cry. 'Ah, you're alive, thank God! Thank God.' She props me up on her lap, where she is sitting on the grass by the roadside. She begins to brush the dirt off me.

'Ma'ami,' I say in a weak voice, 'what happened?'

'Let's just thank God, my husband. We're alive, that's what matters.' Then she shouts out in anger, 'Those crooks!'

My head is aching. But suddenly Ma'ami begins to laugh again. 'Those crooks,' she repeats. 'Just imagine, allowing myself to be caught like that. Me! After all the trouble we had just getting that money. I had to lose it to a couple of small-time crooks, who have probably not stolen any more than ten kobo in their lives. Ah well, we're still alive and unharmed, thank God.'

'They've got the money?'

'Yes, my husband. The thieves, they ripped it from my clothes. You were in front there, you didn't know what was going on. I prayed so hard that you wouldn't turn your head and look back. I was so worried that they might have harmed you. Yes, they searched me all over, the two of them, one holding the knife to my throat. And it was only when they were convinced that it was all I had that they stopped the taxi and flung us out.'

'Thieves...' I am so frightened now that I can't talk again. My teeth are chattering in my mouth. It is completely dark and there are no lights around us anywhere. This makes it even worse for me.

Ma'ami rearranges her clothes as best she can, and then pulls me up.

'Let's go,' she says. 'At least we're alive.' She pats my head to help me get over my fear. 'Fear, my husband! You must learn never to show fear. You're the man of the house, remember? A man must never show that he's afraid.'

We begin to walk. There are no lights on the street in this area but, far ahead, we can see the lights coming from houses, shops and passing vehicles. But there are many other people walking along like us. My fear slowly disappears. Now I am only tired and hungry.

Ma'ami begins to laugh again. I look at her with surprise. The loss of the money is still very painful to me. But Ma'ami bends down and tickles my ribs and shakes me.

'Laugh, my husband. You must learn to laugh. It's the best way to conquer pain. Laugh, and you forget fear. You defeat unhappiness. Ha ha ha! What did I tell you, back there in the market? You remember? Ehn? I'll tell you again. Life, I said, is like the story of the cow and the butchers. Some eat, and some are eaten. And some are there just to watch! You see now? You see why it's so funny?'

She goes on laughing. But then after a few moments she stops abruptly. 'Oh God, my husband, what are we going to do? Where will I find the meat for your birthday tomorrow?'

CHAPTER FOUR

Dejo passes the ball to me. But as I raise my foot to kick it, the ball changes into a snake. I scream, and the snake begins to chase after me, hopping like a toad on short legs.

I run faster. Its tongue darts out and I can see the fangs waiting to bite me. I turn quickly and run another way. I turn again. I run into the house and slam the door shut. The snake is now hurling itself against the wood, threatening to smash it down.

'I know you have no father no father no father,' says the snake, 'and I am going to eat you.'

I shout again, calling to my mother, but when I reach the bed where she is sleeping, she is no longer there. In my terror, I begin to throw the bed covers all about.

And then I wake up, and realise that I have been dreaming. From the next room, I can hear our neighbour's radio talking as it does every morning. The sound must have woken me up as usual, and saved me from the nightmare. I give a deep sigh, happy to have escaped from the snake. I stretch out my hand to touch my mother, and then I jump out of the bed. *Ma'ami is not there!*

I run to the electric switch. The light comes on. But it is true, Ma'ami is not in the room. My heart begins to pound.

I go to the door. The key is in its hole. I stand

staring at it, remembering that Ma'ami always makes sure to take the key out of the door every evening before we go to bed. Slowly I reach forward and try the door. It is open.

I step out, trembling. The only light in the long corridor is the one creeping out from under our neighbour's door. Far down, beyond the door leading out to the backyard, I hear other sounds of people moving around in the early morning – the sound of feet moving, of iron buckets scraping against cement by the water tap, of a man clearing his throat on the street, of distant voices at prayer.

I start to walk to my neighbour's door and then I stop. I decide not to tell her that my mother has disappeared. I tell myself to go outside first and look for myself.

But just as I turn towards the outside door, it opens, and Ma'ami comes in.

'Ma'ami!' I shout, and run towards her. But she waves me back. 'No, my husband. Don't come near me like this. I must have a bath first.'

I do not understand, but I follow her to our room. I watch her take off her clothes and wrap herself in the faded cotton cloth that she always uses as a towel. Then she puts a chewing stick in her mouth, and picks up a bucket. She gathers up the clothes she has just removed, and goes quickly to the backyard.

I follow her, and watch in surprise as she suddenly bends right down to the gutter and begins to vomit.

I shout, and some of our neighbours who are

already in the kitchen run out to Ma'ami. But they stop when they hear her laughter. She tells them that she is all right and nothing is the matter. It was just something she has eaten which has made her sick. They all talk for a few moments and then go back to their work.

Ma'ami throws her clothes into a basin, then carries the basin to the water tap and runs water into it. Then she goes into the bathroom.

I see her hang her wrapper across the bathroom door, and listen to the splash of water on the cement floor. She is not singing today as she usually does.

When she finishes, I am still standing there. So she passes the soap to me, and I go in to have my bath too.

Later, when I return to the room, Ma'ami is already dressed, and there is a strong scent of perfume everywhere. This surprises me, and I don't like the smell at all. But Ma'ami is smiling.

'Come, you can embrace me now, my husband. I want to wish you a happy birthday. I want you to have everything you want!'

'Where did you go?' I ask, pulling out of her arms to get the newly washed clothes that she has placed on the bed for me.

'Why do you want to know? It's my secret.' Then she sees my face. 'Look, must you know everything? Okay, I'll tell you ... but not today. For now, just get ready for school. And, as a special treat, I am going to walk with you to school today. And greet your headmaster. And when you get back, there'll be a huge plate of beef and rice stew waiting on the table here for you, just as I promised!'

'I'm not going to school today,' I say firmly.

'What? What do you mean?'

'I want to stay with you.'

'No, no, my husband. You must not begin to miss school, you know. You have to keep up your good record, remember. We mustn't allow your teacher to start having a bad opinion of you. And besides, how about your sweetheart, Mrs Edun? If she does not see you— '

'I'll explain to her tomorrow. Please let me spend the day with you, Ma'ami.'

'No, sorry, my husband. Besides, I have to go to the market for your meat.'

'I'll go with you.'

'You don't understand. There's not enough money for two bus fares.'

'In that case, I don't want the meat any more!'

I run out of the room and go to the next house, ignoring her calls. When she emerges later, all dressed for the market, I begin to walk along behind her.

She turns angrily to me, pushing the palm of her hand forward to stop me. 'Look, do you know how much I have here? Three naira. And do you know how I got it? I went and washed corpses at the mortuary! Yes, that's what I went to do this morning, to wash dead bodies. I heard someone talk about it last week. They said that they were looking for people to work in the mortuary. So this morning, just to get money, I went ... You know, they pay two naira per body. Two whole naira! I could have made a fortune ... But I tell you, after the first two, I couldn't go on. It was as if the smell was seeping under my skin, into my veins, into my blood. Ah ... I had to run out! Call me a coward, but I just had to get out of that place! I took the four naira I had earned, and went to buy soap and perfume, and ... look, this three naira here is all the money I have left, you hear? If I go alone to the market, then I can still have enough to buy your meat. So I want you to wait for me here until I get back. Please.'

'I still want to come with you,' I say. She looks at me, her lips coming together. Then she walks back to the house to lock the door which she had left open for me.

We take the bus to the meat market, but she does not talk to me. I see her face become angrier and angrier as she pays the fare.

We get to the stalls. They are already crowded with people going to and fro among the wooden tables. They are holding up different chunks of meat in their hands, looking at them carefully, trying to work out the weight and the price.

Ma'ami stands and watches. Then she sighs. 'My husband, why must you always be so stubborn? After the terrible things I had to do in the mortuary, I just have no strength again. It's as if all my inside has been emptied out. So I can't play any games today. I won't be able to convince anybody and we'll just get ourselves into a lot of trouble. Yet we must get your meat, and still pay our fare back.'

We stand a little while longer. She is looking at me, and I am looking elsewhere, biting my lips. Then Ma'ami asks me to wait. She goes to talk to one of the meat sellers who seems to have just made a good sale and is singing to himself.

I don't know what Ma'ami says, but after a while she beckons to me. I follow her behind the butcher's table, to where the waste fat and bones from the meat are being dumped. A crowd of flies rises to meet us, buzzing angrily. But Ma'ami does not hesitate. She bends down and pulls out a bone from the mess. The butcher, at her request, hands her one of his knives, and Ma'ami begins to scrape off the few thin strands of meat still left on the bone.

Then she asks me to bring out all the remaining bones in the dump. I begin to hand them over to her one by one, as she scrapes off the meat. She stops only to hit out at the flies.

We finish at that stall, and go to the next. I pick out the old bones, and she scrapes them with the knife. Then we go on to another stall. We do this for what appears to be a very long time to me, but when I look we have collected just about enough meat to fill my little hand. I am beginning to get tired.

The butchers and cattle traders watch us with amusement, but the first butcher we talked to begins

I pick out the old bones, and she scrapes them with the knife.

to explain to them.

'It's for their dog, I swear,' he says. 'Nowadays, people shop for dogs too, you know.'

The people laugh, and soon they are singing sarcastic songs about us. But Ma'ami ignores them.

Suddenly there is a young man standing in front of my mother. He looks very frightening, with a bushy beard and large, dark spectacles through which you cannot see his eyes. His appearance terrifies me and I move closer to Ma'ami. I am waiting for Ma'ami to shout to me to run.

But the man smiles, and his white teeth flash through his bush of hair. Suddenly he looks kind and friendly, not at all frightening. He says something to Ma'ami, but she shakes her head, meaning that she does not speak English. The man's smile widens and, changing to our language, he apologises to her.

'My dear woman,' he continues, 'please forgive me if it looks as if I am interfering. But we have been watching you for some time, me and my friend in the car over there.' He turns and points. 'That car. You see, I am waiting for my wife who's in the market buying some things. My friend and I have been watching and ... we were wondering if you were in any kind of trouble?'

'Nothing, sir. Because, as you said, it's really not your business, so– '

'No, please, don't misunderstand me, I beg you. I am only asking because ... look, can we help you in any way? We'd very much like to, if you'd let us.'

Suddenly, Ma'ami goes soft, and her voice cracks. 'Sir ... I am tired! Tired of having to beg all the time, begging and begging! My shop ... I lost my shop a long time ago to some of the big people in the government, and ... you see, this is my son here. Today is his birthday. He has not tasted meat for I don't know how many months now. I don't want him to begin to steal. And today, for his birthday, I promised him that ... that ... my dear sir, what is a poor woman to do when she tries and tries but her pockets are dry?'

She is looking at the ground, and I know she is trying not to cry.

The bearded man looks at me and clicks his tongue. He turns and waves at the man in the car. This man, who is wearing a red shirt like one of our teachers at school, climbs quickly out of the car and comes over.

'You see, Eman?' asks the first man. 'It's just as we suspected. The meat is for her son. It's his birthday, and she has no money.'

'Oh dear, this country,' sighs the red shirt. 'What is going to happen to our country? In just a few years we have gone from being rich and happy to ... now look at us, one of the poorest countries in Africa. What kind of beasts are our leaders turning the ordinary people into? Why is it that they just don't care?'

He puts his hand into his pocket. 'Madam, take this. This will not solve all your problems, but at least

I hope it will be enough to give your son a happy birthday! One he won't forget for a long time.'

Ma'ami, her eyes opening wide with surprise and delight, takes the money. It is a twenty naira note! She exclaims and dances.

'And this, from me,' says the bearded man. He leans across the meat table, lifts up a large piece, and asks the butcher to wrap it for me. As he pays, the butcher reaches under the counter, and brings out pieces of steak and liver and some roasted groundnuts. 'I'm adding these, madam, as my own gift to you, to say I am sorry. You didn't say it's your son's birthday, and you allowed us to make those terrible jokes. But it's all right, Allah be praised! Take these for your son, and may it bring me luck!'

'What are you saying?' cries a woman who has come running from opposite us. 'You butchers are so selfish! So you think you're the only one who needs Allah's blessings! Come now, my son! Take these from me, for your birthday!' She places a large leaf on the table, piles it with tomatoes, peppers and onions, and wraps it all up for me.

Soon, before we know it, that section of the market turns into a little bazaar, with the traders and even some customers showering me with gifts. Then they bring some jute and plastic bags and help me pack everything.

I bend down to carry the bags, but find that they are too many and too heavy for me. And for the first

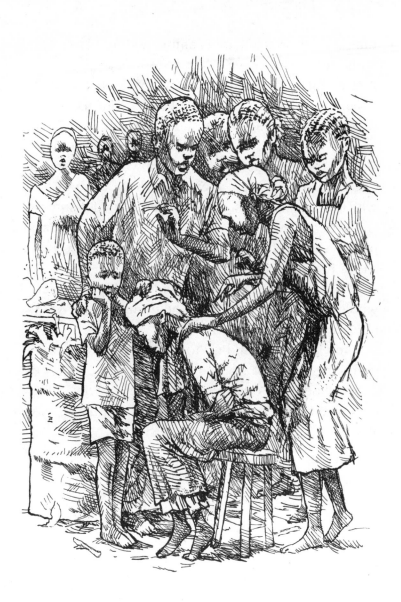

'Oh God, what have I done to deserve such kindness as this?'

time then, I notice that Ma'ami is no longer there with me.

The butchers and traders look everywhere. They shout to each other from stall to stall. Her name is called again and again but there is no answer. There is a feeling of fear in the market and in my stomach. What terrible magic would make a woman disappear?

I am just about to leave when I hear a sound which I recognise. Ma'ami, we discover with surprise, is just behind us, sitting on a low stool by the buzzing pile of waste. Her arms are held across her chest and she is rocking backwards and forwards.

I have seen her cry before, but not like this. Her whole body is shaking, her clothes are soaked with her tears.

They lift her up and try to console her, but the trembling does not stop.

'Oh God, oh God!' she is saying repeatedly. 'Oh God, what have I done to deserve such kindness as this?'

CHAPTER FIVE

Ma'ami calms down at last, and we pick up the bags
of meat and vegetables. After thanking the meat
sellers and the other traders, we start on our journey
home from the market.

Then Ma'ami remembers. We go and search for the
bearded man and his friend in the red shirt, but they
are nowhere to be found. Their car has gone.

Ma'ami is distressed. She says they will never know
now how grateful we are to them.

She raises one of the bags to me. 'You see how life
is, my husband? One moment it is dark and
frightening. You don't know what to do. And then the
next moment, quite suddenly, the sun is shining. You
see, all we need to do is to try to be brave during the
hard times, and they'll pass away! Always remember
that. We must learn not to give in, not to be
frightened. If we are brave and fight on, we can never
lose! Are you listening to me? Even in the middle of
the worst thunderstorm, don't be afraid, because there
comes a time when the weather changes, and the sun
suddenly appears at the end of the road.'

She looks at me, and then bursts out laughing.
'You don't understand. I'm sure all you're thinking
about now is when you're going to eat your meat. I
can see your mouth is watering already.' She pats my
head playfully. 'Don't worry. Just try not to forget

these things I tell you. Some time in the future, you'll find them useful. Especially if, as your mother prays, your life grows richer and you have more chances to do well than I had.'

We find our way through the rows of market stalls and their crowds, and come out on to the tarred road. There is a fine cloud of dust in the air, settling on everything, so that every face we see seems to be freshly powdered.

We reach the bus stop but, surprisingly, Ma'ami does not stop. 'Come, my husband. We'll take the bus, but later. First, there's something we must do.'

She takes my hand, and then she looks at me. I can see that she is thinking. When she speaks, she sounds very serious.

'Listen carefully to what I'm going to say,' she says, 'and repeat it all after me. Are you listening? All right, listen carefully now. "Kindness is like a baton in a relay race. You receive it, and pass it along." Say it.'

I nod my head. 'Kindness,' I say, 'is like a baton in a relay race. When you receive it, you pass it along.'

'Good. I don't want you ever to forget that. Promise me you'll never forget.'

'I promise, Ma'ami.'

I follow her past the Mobil station, towards the railway crossing. We pass a large sign saying VULCANIZER. Then we come to the place where bumps have been erected across the road. Here all vehicles have to slow down, and so it has become the favourite spot of beggars and the smaller hawkers. As usual, they are here now in large numbers, and they try to gather round the cars as they drive slowly over the bumps. They hold out the things they are trying to sell, and they shout the price through the windows of the cars.

Ma'ami pulls me aside and takes out a few coins from her wrapper. She begins to rub the coins all over my head and face. As she does this I look up, and find that she has shut her eyes, and is muttering prayers.

Quickly I shut my eyes too. I listen to her voice as she pleads with the gods to please accept the coins as our offering, because we want to say thanks to them and to our ancestors. She calls her father and her mother to listen from their graves, and asks that the dead do not forget us. She prays that instead they should watch over us every moment of the day, particularly their little grandson. She asks them to take care of me, to keep me safe, and to guide me so that I do nothing bad or foolish. Finally she asks them to help to make me happy and wealthier than she is.

She sighs and opens her eyes. Then she puts the coins in my palms and tells me to go and give them to the beggars. I run forward and do so. But when I finish, the money is not enough, and some of the other beggars crowd round me shouting and calling, their hands held out for more money.

Ma'ami gives me a few more coins, but they are still not enough. More beggars have come running from across the street. They are calling too. They plead for some more money, but Ma'ami pulls me roughly away.

'Kindness must be shared,' she says, 'but we must not be foolish about it!'

We begin to walk again. Soon, however, I begin to feel tired. Also I am getting hungry and cannot take my mind off the meat in the bag I am carrying. But Ma'ami tells me to be patient. She says we will soon have the best meal we have had in months.

As we reach a big roundabout further on down the road, Ma'ami suddenly turns off the main road into a side street. It is a lonely street, with walls and fences and the sound of dogs barking behind the walls. It is a street with very large houses. But it is so silent that I am afraid. I cling to Ma'ami, wondering what we are doing here. Ma'ami has never taken me to any street like this before, where everything is so quiet and frightening and where there is nobody to be seen.

At the end of the street, we begin to turn to the right. But just then Ma'ami suddenly lets out a scream and pulls me tight against her bosom, my face crushed into her waist. I hear the sound of a car as it comes by, and of an iron gate grinding open. I am unable to see, and my heart is beating wildly against my ribs. Ma'ami seems to be as frightened as I am. After a while, I hear her sigh. Her breathing drops back to normal, and she releases me. But as we begin to walk again, she holds on to my arm.

Then she taps me softly on the shoulder, making a sign with her head so that I look to the side. I see a big car coming to a stop by some flower pots inside the compound of a house. There is a high wall and big gates which a watchman is holding open. I can see a large white house with tall windows. I can see a place with tables and chairs outside and the whole house is shining brightly in the sunshine.

Ma'ami leans sideways and whispers, 'Look carefully, my husband, as we walk past.'

I keep on looking, and see a short fat man literally roll out of the car. His hair is cut very short, and he seems to have no neck. He has a light complexion, which is made to look even lighter by the flowing white lace *agbada* that he is wearing.

As I look, he bends down and reaches back inside the car. He lifts out a small suitcase, and then what looks like a walking stick. The watchman runs and shuts the door of the car, which now drives on to somewhere beyond my vision around the back of the house.

The man turns and begins to climb up the steps to the entrance of the white-painted house. And then I notice the other person with him. This person must have stepped down from the other side of the car. It is a woman, about the same height as the man. She is wearing a light-coloured *buba*, with a green *gele* and wrapper. She is slim and walks like a young person. I cannot see her face, however, because she has her back to the road.

Then the tall gates swing closed again, blocking out the scene.

'Look carefully, my husband, as we walk past.'

'Did you see him?' asks Ma'ami. There is a strange note in her voice, which I don't understand.

But I nod. 'Yes, I saw the man very well. But the woman, I couldn't see her face.'

Ma'ami gives a strange laugh. 'That's all right. It's *him* I wanted you to see.' There is a pause. Then she says, 'He's your father.'

My heart almost stops beating. 'My ... my ... father!' I feel like shouting. Then I feel like crying. Then I feel as if I am choking. Then I feel everything at once.

My father? My father! My ... oh God! That man! The man I've just seen? How, how? Is that him, the father I've always longed to know, to see, to touch, to hold ... oh God, help me, help me.

That's the father I thought I never had, because Ma'ami would never speak of him. At last.

'Let's go back,' I hear myself cry out. 'Ma'ami, please take me back. I want to see him again. I want–' I don't say the rest. I feel somehow that it will hurt Ma'ami if I tell her I want my father to hold me, to carry me on his shoulders. Oh, just to touch me!

But Ma'ami is shaking her head. 'No, my husband.' Tears are flowing freely down her cheeks. 'I know how you feel, but believe me, he doesn't wish to see either you or me again. I left him, years ago, and he said that if I left I was never to return. I'm sure he has forgotten us by now. And he has someone else to look after him.'

She unfolds the edge of her wrapper, and wipes

my eyes with the cloth, though her own eyes are even more wet than mine. But her voice has grown stronger and more steady now as she speaks.

'You're ten today,' she says quietly, 'and that's why I brought you past here. To show you his house, so you know you have a father, and that he is still alive ... I didn't know that we'd be so lucky, that he would turn up just at the right moment for you to see him. So now you know. I'm happy. One day, you'll be able to decide for yourself, whether you wish to go back to him, or make your own separate way in life ... But now, let's go back and cook your meat!'

We walk back past the houses again, and I note the number on the locked gate.

We soon get back to the main street again, and have to wait as there is no bus. I find myself looking back again and again, to see if the big car will drive out with my father in it. Ma'ami plucks a leaf from a flower nearby, and puts it in her mouth. She is looking at me in a way I have never seen her look before. Then she comes towards me and runs her fingers softly through my hair and down the back of my neck.

'My husband ... you're still young, and I doubt if you'll understand any of it. But one day, I promise you, you'll hear the whole story, from the beginning. All that I've been through since I married your father.'

She pauses briefly, her eyes clouded up. Then she resumes. 'You see, your father ... you saw his big car, and his big house. You saw his rich woman, one of the several that he has now. He is rich, yes, very, very rich. But he wasn't always like this. When I met him, he was just an ordinary man ...'

She sighs heavily. 'Yes, I left him when I knew that the things he was doing were really bad. It was ... it was too much for me! I wasn't going to tell on him or start a scandal. I had decided to leave him to his God and his conscience. I couldn't live with him any more. So one day I packed my box, put you on my back, and decided to walk out. I thought that would frighten him, bring him back to his senses. But no! He pushed us out and slammed the door. Yes, slammed the door in our faces, shouting words I dare not repeat.

'And I turned and walked away. Yes, with these two feet, I walked away from his house and out of his life. And even then, I was still praying for him, still hoping, but ... Ah, if that's how to be rich in this world, if that's what a person has to do to get money, then please, little husband, I want none of it. Let me remain poor, like this, or even worse if that is my fate. Let me continue to suffer as I am doing. A free life and a good, clear conscience is better than all the wealth of this world ...'

I can see that her thoughts are far away now, as if she is looking at some picture deep in her mind. Then her eyes come back to me.

'My husband, this is what we've been paying for all these years. Because I refused to follow your father on the terrible road he chose. He would not turn back, he was deaf to my pleas. Then he could not forgive me for leaving him. He felt hurt, and he thought he must hurt me too ... and you, of course. Not only did he turn his back completely on us, but he made sure, as he became more important, as he joined the big people, that he stopped me wherever I turned. That's why it's been so hard. For I had nothing when I agreed to go with him, nothing except my foolish love for him.

'I left school because of him, broke away from my guardians, my relatives, my friends. And for the nine years that followed, I lived on my pride, and survived. Or so I thought ... until one day ... Ah, my husband, I'll tell you more later. But listen to me. All that I suffered, all the pain I had, does not matter. Pain tests us, it makes us strong! One day, yes, one day you're going to be bigger than him!'

I do not understand all of it. I do not understand at all. I do not understand and I am hurt. What reason does she think she can give me? How can she explain why she has kept me away so cruelly, and for so long, from my father? All the jokes and beatings at school and on our street because I do not have a father. The bag in my hands feels heavy, but I do not wish to eat any meat now.

CHAPTER SIX

When the bus arrives, I am still not able to speak to Ma'ami. I keep seeing the image of the man she calls my father, and each image makes him more beautiful in my eyes.

Ma'ami is talking, explaining, occasionally sobbing, but all I know is that I wish to see my father. I want to jump on his lap, throw my arms round his neck, take him to see my friends in the school and the jeering boys and girls along our street.

All those stupid boys who have been abusing me for so long, calling me terrible names because I have no father. I want now to show my father to them, show them his big car, the car that their own fathers haven't got, and show them his big, beautiful house, which none of their fathers will ever have.

I want to sing, too, as they have been singing, with my head in the air, as everybody trembles before my father. Oh, why has Ma'ami been so cruel, hiding my father from me like this all these years? I listen to Ma'ami, but I do not hear a word of what she is saying. I have made up my mind what I am going to do. When the bus arrives, I will let Ma'ami get in first, and pretend that I am about to follow her inside. Then, as soon as the bus is about to leave, I will jump out and run away. I will go and see my father.

Everything seems to clear up in my mind as soon as I come to this decision. I am no longer worried or sad. In fact, I begin to smile. Now I can hear what Ma'ami is saying.

'Children,' she shakes her head. 'They don't understand. They don't see the world as it really is. They don't remember anything. They don't remember what it was like before. What a great pity.'

I say nothing. I am watching the bus as it appears from up the street, coming towards us. As it grows larger, I go over the plan in my head. Then I tell myself that this is the right thing to do. The bus is closer now. I tell myself that the moment is coming when I will free myself from this woman and be united with my long-lost father.

The bus stops, and the usual rush begins as several people struggle to climb in. But Ma'ami does not move. I look up at her with alarm. She is looking at me with a sad expression on her face. Is it possible that she has read my mind?

Suddenly she takes my hand and pulls me away from the crowd.

'Come. I think I know what's going on in your mind, my poor little husband. Come with me. I think there's something you ought to see. Perhaps it will help you to understand.'

I follow her, but the anger is beginning to fill my mind again. I want to be with my father at last. Can't she understand that? How can a person live without a father? How can one live with the laughter and the jeers of playmates?

'My husband,' Ma'ami is speaking. 'I raised you.

Suddenly she takes my hand and pulls me away from the crowd.

You ripened here in my womb. These hands fed you, washed you, nursed you through good health and bad. I know every part of your body as well as I know my own. And so I can also read your mind. There's no need for you to pretend with me, you hear? Say it out. Tell me that you're angry. Tell me what you want. You have been with me all these years, but it's still your father you wish to go to. Isn't that the truth?'

I keep quiet. I know that I cannot admit it, but if I try to lie she will find out the truth in my voice. For the first time in my life, I find that the pain in her voice does not make me want to cry for her.

'It's all right,' she sighs. 'Whatever is going to happen will happen. There's nothing we can do to stop it. Is that the reward mothers get for loving their children? Perhaps it is right that a son returns to his father in the end, no matter what we do to keep him.'

'Ma'ami,' I begin. I want to apologise, to explain to her, to make her understand. I want to tell her that it is not what she thinks. Going to my father does not mean my going away from her or that I do not love her. But all I find myself saying is, 'Ma'ami, why can't you go back to Father? Why can't both of you live together again?'

'Me and your father, live together! After all I've been telling you.'

She stops in the street, and stands quite still. Everything else seems to stop too. There is a long silence. Then we begin to walk again, and all the

64

sounds of the world come back to my ears.

For a while, however, Ma'ami says nothing more. Then I notice that we have got near my father's house again.

We arrive close to the gate. Ma'ami unwraps her *gele*, and folds it round her head and face, the way Muslim women do. Then she knocks on the gate.

The watchman we saw before opens a peephole and puts his head out.

My mother greets him and asks, 'Is *oga* in?'

Yes,' answers the watchman, looking suspiciously at us. 'What do you want?'

'Please, it's my son. They say they want him to come and clear the garden and wash the kitchen.'

'Ah, madam,' the watchman's eyes go round like a piece of kola nut. He looks again at Ma'ami, and seems about to say something. Then he scratches his head, and looks back furtively at the house. His head leans out further from the gate, as he whispers, 'I swear, madam, I like you. So please take this advice I am giving you, in the name of Allah! Your son, take him away quickly! Don't bring him here! Go quickly!'

Ma'ami looks at me. Then she turns to the watchman and raises her voice. 'What did you say? I don't unders– '

'Sh! Ssshhh! Look, it's on your own head!' Quickly the watchman draws back and goes to open the little door in the gate.

'I was saying I didn't hear what you– '

'Nothing! Nothing, in the name of Allah! Go inside

and find out for yourself, but don't get me into trouble.'

There is a frightened look in his eyes, and I wonder if Ma'ami has seen it. It makes me feel proud, for I am sure it is my father who inspires such fear in this man. Ah, so my father is very powerful. I am excited! I just can't wait to leap into his arms.

But Ma'ami is whispering to me. 'Careful, don't make too much noise, you hear? Let's go as quietly as possible.'

She pulls me off the gravel path, and we continue on the grass. I walk behind her, trying to peer around her wrapper.

From the back, Ma'ami looks rather different now to me. She is carrying the bags in the crook of her left arm. Her *gele* is draped over her head and shoulders, her head bent forward. Somehow her walk has changed, and she seems to have developed a limp.

We walk around the house, to the back. There is nobody in sight, only three big Mercedes Benz cars, all of the same dark blue colour. Ma'ami leads me past them to a path to the left of the garage, lined with well-trimmed hibiscus and small palms.

'Aren't we going into the house?' I ask. But Ma'ami hushes me quickly, with a warning finger to her lips. 'Don't talk. We're not safe yet.'

She points. Ahead of us is a clump of banana trees, with a small brick house to the right of them.

'There, my husband,' Ma'ami says in a whisper, 'right inside there, is where we used to live.'

My heart begins to thump, but Ma'ami smiles. 'The house is empty now. It's been empty since the new, bigger house behind us was built. I think they only use it as a kind of store-house now. But come, that's not what I want to show you ...'

Ma'ami looks around quickly, and then steps through a space in a thick hedge. We head for the clump of banana trees.

'If we're lucky, and they haven't changed their habits, then the old man who guards this place won't be there now. He'll be taking a nap in his room in the boys' quarters.'

We stop behind one of the palms. Ma'ami whispers to me to act as if I have a thorn in my foot. As I do so, she bends with me, as if to help remove the thorn. Everything is so mysterious to me and I am dying to ask questions.

Ma'ami drops my foot and straightens up. 'Good, he's not there. Let's hurry!'

She pulls me into the banana grove, and suddenly we come face to face with a small square building, painted white. It is in fact more like a big box of cement, for it has no windows at all, and the only door I can see has a huge rusted lock dangling on it.

Ma'ami turns and begins to examine the hundreds of pieces of pottery of all sizes which I now notice are scattered around the ground. Then she grunts, reaches forward, and lifts one of them. Under it is a key. Ma'ami picks it up with a smile of triumph, and opens the door.

What I see next is like a scene in one of the frightening tales our teacher occasionally tells us. There is a table against the wall, and on top of it is a tangled heap of bones and skulls. At one end of the table is a solitary candle, half-burnt.

The glow of the candle gives off a very feeble light, but I am still able to see the smears of blood everywhere, and fresh blood too from its smell. My head goes round in a sudden whirl and I think I am going to faint. But my eyes clear again and I start to turn away to the door.

But as I turn, trying to reach for Ma'ami, I suddenly notice something else at the corner of the room. It is a figure kneeling. It is a small naked boy, with a calabash balanced on his head. He is staring at the floor, unblinking, and he has a chain of cowries around his legs.

It is lucky that Ma'ami is looking at me just at that moment, so that she is able to clamp her hand quickly across my mouth and cut off my scream.

She pulls me out and shuts the door. My head is still swimming.

'Let's run,' she whispers in my ear, and then pulls me back again. 'Wait, wait! Let me spoil it for them first.'

She flings the door open again, and runs inside to where the boy is kneeling. She grabs the calabash, and throws it on the floor. Then she runs out again and bangs the door.

She is breathing heavily. I still feel weak and I am

I suddenly notice something else at the corner of the room.

struggling to steady my eyes. 'It's too late for the boy, but at least they won't gain a thing from it. And I hope his blood damns them for ever!'

She looks at me where I am leaning against one of the banana trees. 'You see for yourself now, my husband, the evil in this place?'

'Let's ... let's go, Ma'ami! Let's get away.'

'All these years ... you know, I was half-praying, all the time we were coming, that all this would have ended, that you wouldn't see this terrible bad side of your father. You poor thing. But can you imagine how I felt that first day I came here myself, and found my own son kneeling there ...'

'Your son, Ma'ami?'

'Yes, my son, our first son, who would have been your elder brother ... there, with a calabash on his head!' Her voice has fallen into a whisper. 'Ah, what money will do to people in this world! I'd gone to hospital, to have you. But I was allowed to go home quite early since I had no problems at all, and I was strong ... I came home. Your father was away and there was no one around. So I came to the garden, saw this building I hadn't seen before, and came to look ... Ah, let me stop there ... His own son! The fruit of my womb! Just for money ... How could anyone do that to their own son, even for money? I would have snatched him up but by then it was too late. I couldn't save him. His spirit had gone.'

We both seem to hear the noise at the same time. Voices cursing, feet running towards the grove, the

70

furious barking of a dog. I look up in panic. But Ma'ami is calm.

'They're coming,' she says grimly. 'They're coming to catch us, the fools! Just like the last time. They don't know who they are dealing with.'

CHAPTER SEVEN

Ma'ami runs quickly to the wall of banana trees. She pushes the leaves aside with her hands and looks through.

'The men are no problem,' she says as she turns towards me. 'Only three of them, and one is an idiot. But the dogs ...'

She straightens up, looking at me, and then her face changes. She exclaims, 'Oh, of course! Look at me! I'm getting old and forgetful.'

She rushes to the back of the fence, snaps off the branch of one of the creepers, then bends and tears off some other leaves. Tying them together as quickly as she can, she puts them between her palms, and rubs them together violently. Then she runs to the path the approaching men and dogs will take, and throws the bunch of twigs and leaves down on the ground.

She grabs my arm. 'Come, my little husband, let's get away!'

We run round the small white building and Ma'ami pulls me through a gap in the banana fence. As we run on the grass towards the far end of the outer wall, I hear the barking of the dogs suddenly cease behind us, and change into low moans. They begin to wail now, as dogs usually do at night when, as the boys say, they see a ghost passing.

'Quick!' snaps Ma'ami. 'Behind the water tank!'

There is a clothes line behind the tank, with some clothes hanging over it. Just behind one of the poles supporting the line Ma'ami reaches out and pulls at the wall. Five or six bricks fall out and there, right in front of us, is a rough round hole, where the bricks have been loosened, to make way to the street outside.

Ma'ami lifts me up with one hand and pushes me though the hole. Then she throws the bags in a heap at me. As I am not ready to catch them, they fall to the ground around me, spilling out their contents.

I bend down to retrieve the bags, while Ma'ami puts her right foot out first, and then quickly wriggles the rest of her body out to where I am standing. She grabs the bags from my hands, and we begin to run up the street.

Finally, judging the danger over, we stop by a lamp post. We are panting heavily, both of us.

Then Ma'ami begins to laugh softly. 'Fools! Fools!' She says this repeatedly, the sound building up in her throat like the ring of bells. Her hair is all dishevelled, her *buba* badly torn, but Ma'ami is laughing.

When she stops, I ask her the question that has been bothering me.

'Ah yes, those leaves!' she answers. 'That's something I learnt from my grandfather on the farm, long ago. Yes, that's where I grew up, on the farm. You see, my mother's father, your great-grandfather, he was a farmer, and a hunter. Pity he died before you were born. You wouldn't believe all the things he taught me. He was unhappy that his only grandchild was a girl, but still, he taught me as much as he thought I should know. And the knowledge of plants was one of them. One day, I hope I'll have time to teach you too.'

'I want to know things, Ma'ami. I want to learn.'

'You will ... if you stay with me.'

'I'm staying with you! I'm not going away again. I won't be stupid, ever again.'

'Well, we'll see. Plants! You see, some plants are normally chosen for gardens, to drive away dangerous snakes. But there are different types of these, and I myself, I planted many of them years ago in your father's house. Now, two of them are peculiar. If you crush them together, or at least rub them so that their saps mix, you can use the mixture to tame dogs or cure rabies! Just the smell of it is enough. No dog will come near within a mile! No, they'll be running with their tails behind their legs. Good thing I remembered just in time ... and that hole in the wall too! If you knew how many times I tried to have it blocked up, when I was mistress of the house, and how many times the servants kept reopening it! Somehow I just knew it would still be there ...'

I am just about to ask other questions, about my father whom I hate so much now, when something like a vice grips my arm. Startled, I cry out in pain, and Ma'ami swivels round.

I look, and there is a man towering above me, with

a frightful face and red eyes. He is swinging a long machete in his other hand.

'Come quietly with me,' hisses the man, 'or I'll kill you!'

I open my mouth to shout again, but the sound chokes in my throat as I see his face again and remember him. It is the watchman from my father's house.

Ma'ami throws herself down at his feet and holds on to his ankles. But the man kicks his feet free, still dragging me along. 'Stop screaming, boy! I say, stop screaming! Or I'll cut your head off, with this!' The big machete gleams in his fist. 'And you, woman robber, out of my way!'

We go on shouting like this for a time, while he kicks and drags us along the ground.

Then, abruptly, Ma'ami stops her wailing. She steps in front of the watchman, and faces him angrily.

I hear her spit and say, 'Look at you!' Then she gives a long hiss and spits again, snapping at the man in words I don't understand. I know from the sound that this is Hausa language, but never before have I heard Ma'ami speak it, and I am completely astonished to hear her now speaking as fluently as any of the women in Sabo.

'*Ashe kaima dayan sune!* [So you are one of them!] *Ka kaimu wurin su, su kashe mu!* [Take us to them, then, so they may kill us!]'

She has folded her arms across her chest, a look of disgust and hatred on her face. She continues: '*Dama*

76

She steps in front of the watchman and faces him angrily.

maigidanka ma ya saba kashe yara don kudi! [Your master is used to killing children for money!] *Kuma duk ya'yan talakawa ne, kamar kai da ni.* [For they are all children of the poor, like you and me.]'

Then she concludes: '*To, amma wataran Allah zai nuna muku!* [Well, one day God will show you!]'

It is as if someone has struck the watchman a violent blow across the face. I see him shiver, as he hurriedly releases my arm.

'*Karya ne* [It's a lie], madam!' he says to Ma'ami, who is now standing on one foot and using the big toe of the other one to draw patterns on the sand. '*Ni ba dayan su bane!* [I'm not one of them!]'

His voice grows even louder as he tries to explain to Ma'ami. I still do not know what he is saying, but he wants Ma'ami to believe him. '*Kitunafa, na gargade ku kada kushigo cikin gidan!* [Remember, I advised you not to enter the house!] *Idan mu talakawa bamu tsaya tare ba, ta yaya zamu rayu?* [If we the poor do not stand together, how shall we survive?]'

He searches in his pocket and brings out a sweet which is half-crushed already. He tries to smooth it, then presses it into my hand. He turns and begins to walk away.

'*Kutafi, ke da danki.* [Go, you and your son.] *Zan gayawa maigidana cewa ni ban ganku ba. Allah ya kiyaye!* [I'll tell my master that I didn't see you. May God protect you!]'

And then he is gone. Ma'ami sighs. 'It's always the

same story, unfortunately. We who are poor, if only we could stick together sometimes! If only we realised how powerful we could be. If we just stayed together and did things together or spoke with one great voice!'

We begin to walk away again. 'Ma'ami, what did you tell him? Why did he just walk away like that? And was that Hausa you were speaking?'

'Yes, it was Hausa. Ah yes, I remember, you've never heard me speak it.' She smiles. 'There's still so much to tell you, about your mother! Well, one day, you'll know everything ... When my grandfather died, one of his older sons took me to the north, to Kaduna. That's where I began to trade, and learnt that if you work in the market, you have to speak many languages.'

She breaks off, and I know she is thinking of something. I wait, and then ask her again what she told the watchman.

'I told him to do his worst, that's all. I pointed out to him that he and I are the same kind of people, even if he does not realise it. We are both poor people who have to work for the rich. We are in the hands of the rich. Then I reminded him of his belief in Allah. God is always watching and will make us pay in the end for all our sins, whether we are just doing what we are told or not. It frightened him, as I thought it would. He is really a good man ... you remember that he tried to warn us against going into the house. Now he's going to tell his master that he didn't find us. It's not often that poor people help each other. We're always so busy trying to please rich people.' She laughs, then casts a hurried look backwards.

She takes my hand. 'Let's hurry up now and get away from this street!'

I ask my next question when we arrive at the bus stop.

'How does what they were doing to that little boy make them rich?'

She stands at the bus stop looking down at me. I can tell that she is trying to find a way to explain it to me.

'It's not the magic rituals which make them rich, as many people think. People come to him to do the magic for them, but they know that magic has nothing to do with it. The terrible thing is that it makes your father rich.

'No matter how many poor children they kidnap and kill, they all know that, to make their quick money, they still must cheat and cheat. They must lie and steal, steal and lie. They cheat their friends and the state. It is by cheating and lying that they fill their fat stomachs.

'The evil rituals do not make them richer. I think that these magic rituals and killings and sacrifices help to make them tougher, these so-called big men. It helps to toughen them, so they don't behave like human beings again. They become greedier and greedier. They need more money, and they love the power the money gives them. So they sell themselves completely to the devil, till they can no longer turn back. It's terrible, my husband.

'Never worship money, my little husband. If you begin to worship it, money turns you into a beast! One day, one day, we must get rid of all the evil, crazy people who are destroying our lives. We must fight them, make our society happy and clean again. The decent people want to breathe freely and without fear.'

She stops and then shakes her head sadly. She puts her arm around my shoulders and holds me close to her. She gives a long sigh.

'When I look at you young people, you who are younger than us ... all these boys and girls who have gone to school with you, I get frightened. I am afraid, afraid! They all seem to act in the same way as their fathers. They laugh and jeer at you because you can't point to your father. They fight and hurt one another. They will steal without shame. Perhaps the evil has gone too deep into their blood, or perhaps ...'

The bus arrives before she can finish her statement. For a moment she is going to say something more, but then she smiles and turns to the bus. We climb in, this time without much trouble as there are only a few people about.

Inside the bus, a singing session is going on. Everyone seems to have stopped singing just while the bus was picking up its new passengers. As soon as we are seated, the song starts up again.

It is a popular song, one that is normally sung at Christmas in praise of Mary the Virgin Mother because of her suffering for her son, but nobody seems to notice or care that we are not in the Christmas season. Everybody is singing lustily, some the Yoruba version, some the Igbo words, and some the English. There is great joy in the bus, almost as if everyone is trying to forget some pain, to shut out the outside world. The singing is not very good, and some of the passengers are not sure of the right tune. But everyone is singing so happily that Ma'ami joins them too. She tries to get me to sing by tickling my ribs.

I don't feel like singing at all. I do not have a very good singing voice, and I do not join in as quickly as Ma'ami does. But she will not leave me alone, and keeps pinching my ribs. So when they come to the part that I know, I smile and sing with them: 'Hallelujah! Hallelujah! Christ is born today ...'

When I finish singing that with them, I sit quietly watching the driver. Ma'ami seems satisfied. I go on listening to them, humming at those moments where I remember the tune. Perhaps that is the reason why I am the only one on the bus who hears the driver cursing angrily as we approach a road-block mounted by soldiers and policemen.

'These people again!' I hear the driver talking out loud to himself. 'Will they never be satisfied? I gave them something just two hours ago, the last time I passed them. But look, they're waving to me again, to stop! Just how much do I make, to be bribing them every time I pass a road-block? Well, not this time! I'm not going to stop!'

The bus has been slowing down, but suddenly it picks up speed. The driver accelerates and drives straight at the road-block. I look through the window of the bus, and I see the caps and guns of the policemen and the soldiers dancing in the sun as they leap out of the way. I see one of them raise his hand and shout something. But the singing in the bus drowns his voice and I cannot hear what he is saying.

The driver is laughing. 'Crooks! Cheats! Robbers!'

Then there is a sudden explosion at the back of the bus. The singing abruptly stops. Almost at the same moment, the bus starts to turn over on its side, throwing everybody forward out of their seats. There is the splintering of glass above the screaming voices, and the bus smashes with a thundering crash into a lamp post. I find myself flying through the window, with a piece of someone's clothing in my hands.

I don't remember landing anywhere, but suddenly there are several bodies pushing and pressing around me, as I try to struggle up, shouting for Ma'ami. Hands, many hands, are clutching at me, and I cannot see clearly through my tears. The smell of blood and petrol is inside my nostrils.

So many voices are shouting, crying, sobbing. A crowd has appeared from nowhere and they are standing and pointing. They talk excitedly to one another. With all my strength I push my way through the crowd, searching desperately.

I shout for Ma'ami, but the only sounds are the crying of the women and the shouts of the men. The sound of my own voice echoes in my head.

The *danfo* bus we were travelling in is nothing now but a tangle of iron and steel. It is lying over on one side, its door torn open, and some bodies are being pulled out of it. I run forward, screaming. And then I see her.

She is lying untidily across the front seat, tangled with some other bodies. Her *gele* has fallen off, revealing an ugly mess of red and white and dripping blood, where the bullets have torn into her skull.

'Ma'ami!' I shout, running forward, but strong hands hold me back.

'They fired! They fired into the bus!' the voices are crying as they pull the bodies out.

'Yes! They said the driver refused to stop!'

'Oh God! Oh God! Look at the dead bodies!'

I am looking at Ma'ami, calling her name. But she is not answering back. I call again.

Someone is shaking me, speaking to me. I do not listen and try to struggle away. 'Ma'ami!' I cry once more.

Then the words are louder, close to my ear. 'Come away, my little husband. More soldiers are coming! Quickly!'

'Ma'ami!' I turn around. I turn my back on the woman tangled across the front seat, her *gele* so like Ma'ami's and now stained with blood.

I hide my face against Ma'ami, my eyes tightly

'Ma'ami!' I shout, running forward.

shut. I am empty and cold and so weak that I cannot stand.

'Come! Quickly!' Her arms are supporting me. She helps me walk, though she herself is limping badly.

I do not notice where we go. I do not know how long we have been walking.

'Ma'ami ...' Now I am stronger, though I find I have small pains here and there, and cuts from the bus window.

'Ah, my little husband!' She stops and looks at me. Blood is trickling down her face. She shakes her head. 'We have lost everything. Again we have nothing. And it's your birthday!'

I hold on to her tightly. 'That is nothing now, Ma'ami.'

We walk on.

Discussion

1 'When the rich commit a crime they often get away with it, but when the poor commit a crime they are almost always caught.' How true do you think this statement is?

2 We still hear about witch doctors at football matches and during elections, and children still disappear in mysterious circumstances. How big a part does witchcraft play in countries in Africa?

3 For people in many countries in Africa, life is becoming more, rather than less, difficult. Why is this happening and what can be done about it?

Glossary of Yoruba words

(The page numbers are for the first reference)

agbada (page 55) traditional gown for men

boole (page 31) roasted plantain

buba (page 5) woman's traditional blouse

eba (page 3) mashed cassava

gele (page 3) woman's head-tie

mama ibeji (page 18) mother of twins

oga (page 65) boss, master of the house

Other books in the Junior African Writers Series

Level 5

Travellers

Keith Whiteley

Three short stories. The travellers are Thina, Tebogo and Nonkosi, children of Africa. In a violent land they face danger and fear. But they also find love and kindness, and a new understanding. Their journeys do not take them far, but by the end their lives are changed for ever.

0 435 89365 3   112pp

Taxi!

Barbara Kimenye

The guilt and shame of a hit-and-run driver. Paulo, the taxi driver, accidentally runs over his friend's son, and trouble follows him wherever he goes. Can he ever make amends?

0 435 89363 7   112pp

The Cruel War

Kwasi Koranteng

Set in a brutal civil war in Liberia, this is a love story about two young people trying to escape the horrors of their situation.

0 435 89361 0   128pp

Cry Softly, Thule Nene

Shirley Bojé

The world of Thule Nene is turned upside-down when her family is killed in a brutal bloodbath. She is sent to a poor orphanage, with little hope for the future. Then she is offered a new start with a wealthy family, if she will help to look after a crippled white girl.

0 435 89358 0   128pp

The Junior African Writers Series is designed to provide interesting and varied African stories either for pleasure or for study. There are five graded levels in the series at present.

Level 5 is the upper level in the series. It is aimed at more mature young adults and advanced readers who are looking for material which is challenging but still controlled for language and content.

Content The stories will appeal to anyone who wants to read about problems facing young people in contemporary society in Africa. At this level the series does not hesitate to ask readers to think hard, nor, occasionally, to shock them into looking again at what is happening around them.

Language Authors are encouraged to use language more freely and more evocatively than in the other levels. The basic vocabulary is about 2250 words, but new words, essential to the development of the story or just right for a particular situation, are introduced. Every attempt is made to contextualise them and they are repeated through the story. Sentence length is less controlled, but very difficult or very complex sentences are avoided.

Dictionary Difficult words which readers do not know and which are not made clear in the illustrations or the context of the story should be looked up in a dictionary. This will help develop dictionary skills and will ensure the reader's full enjoyment of the story.

Discussion At this level, discussion of some of the issues examined in the story will be much more useful to the reader than comprehension questions and activities. The discussion can be carried out in the classroom or among friends.